Good Baby

Nanette Newman

and Jonathan Langley

Collins

An imprint of HarperCollins*Publishers*

Good Baby is so unbelievably good,

she always does everything just as she should.

She smiles really
nicely and always
says 'Please'.

She likes to look
smart and never
would tease.

She's never been whiney or wailed or been sick.

When playing with Freddie she gives him the stick.

And never - no NEVER -
hangs on and says 'NO'
when the poor little
puppy is wanting it so.

She drinks all her milk,
never spits it about.

Her voice is so
gentle you won't
hear her shout.

She piles up the bricks,
doesn't knock
them
all
down.

She uses her potty
before going to town.

She sits very quietly and just nods her head.
She doesn't drive everyone mad before bed.

She won't break
her toys or throw
them away.

She kisses her
aunty when she
comes to stay.

She doesn't get
dirty or mess up
her hair,

and all of her books
she is happy to share.

She's kind to her cat and goes 'Aaah' when he's near
and when she's told 'No', there is never a tear.

She plays very gently
with her best friend, Paul.
She doesn't like rough games
or pushing at all.

She loves doing jigsaws and makes sure each bit
is put in its place and really does fit.

I have to admit it, she's sweet through and through.
She's always so cuddly and smiley, it's true.

Shall I say it?
Well, should I?
Are you wondering who?

I think that this baby just has to be . . .

YOU!

YOU!

I'm sure this baby isn't like . . .

She's cheeky and naughty and quite shouty too,

We beg and we plead but she just makes a noise.

When it's time for her bath
she grizzles some more
and throws all her things
in a heap on the floor.

She won't leave her games or pick up her toys.

She unwinds the knitting
and tears all the books.

She screams when
she's sitting and
gives nasty looks.

She never says 'Please', she just grabs and says 'More'.

She tips bowls on her head and throws jam on the floor.

I have to admit it, she just can't be good.
She doesn't do anything quite as she should.

She'll climb in the dustbin and give it a lick.

She'll swallow some paper and then be quite sick.

She'll snatch all the toys and twist Bunny's ear.
She'll dribble and gobble and snarl and then sneer.

And after all that - as if that's
not enough - she'll get out
the paint box and paint
Archie's cuff!

She'll butter her hair and screw up her nose.
She'll snort like a pig and bite Archie's toes.

She'll growl at
the cat and hide
Daddy's money.

She'll smack 'dearest Teddy'
and think it's all funny.

She'll yell for more biscuits
when she's given cake.

She'll comb Nana's
hair with the old
garden rake.

She'll break all
the cups. She'll spit
on the floor.

She'll crawl in the cupboard
and write on the door.

When she wakes from her nap with a scowl and a moan,
'Oh no, it's **Bad Baby**,' you'll hear us all groan.

Bad Baby

Nanette Newman
and Jonathan Langley

First published in Great Britain by HarperCollins Publishers Ltd in 2003

1 3 5 7 9 10 8 6 4 2

Paperback ISBN-13: 978-0-00-786733-2

Text copyright © Nanette Newman 2003 Illustrations copyright © Jonathan Langley 2003
The HarperCollins website address is: www.harpercollins.co.uk
Printed in China